the pros & cons of being a frog

for marta and claude

SIMON & SCHUSTER BOOKS FOR YOUNG READERS
An imprint of Simon & Schuster Children's Publishing Division
1230 Avenue of the Americas, New York, New York 10020
Copyright © 2012 by Sue deGennaro
Originally published in Australia in 2012 by Scholastic Australia Pty Limited
First US edition 2016
All rights reserved, including the right of reproduction in whole or in part in any form.
SIMON & SCHUSTER BOOKS FOR YOUNG READERS is a trademark of Simon & Schuster, Inc.
For information about special discounts for bulk purchases, please contact Simon & Schuster
Special Sales at 1-866-506-1949 or business@simonandschuster.com.
The Simon & Schuster Speakers Bureau can bring authors to your live event.
For more information or to book an event, contact the Simon & Schuster Speakers Bureau
at 1-866-248-3049 or visit our website at www.simonspeakers.com.
The text for this book was set in Fragment Core
The illustrations for this book were rendered in collage, Conté crayons, pencil, and ink.
Manufactured in China
0616 SCP
2 4 6 8 10 9 7 5 3 1
CIP data for this book is available from the Library of Congress.
ISBN 978-1-4814-7130-5
ISBN 978-1-4814-7131-2 (eBook)

Sue deGennaro

the pros & cons of being a frog

A Paula Wiseman Book
Simon & Schuster Books for Young Readers
New York London Toronto Sydney New Delhi

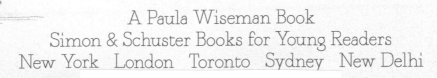

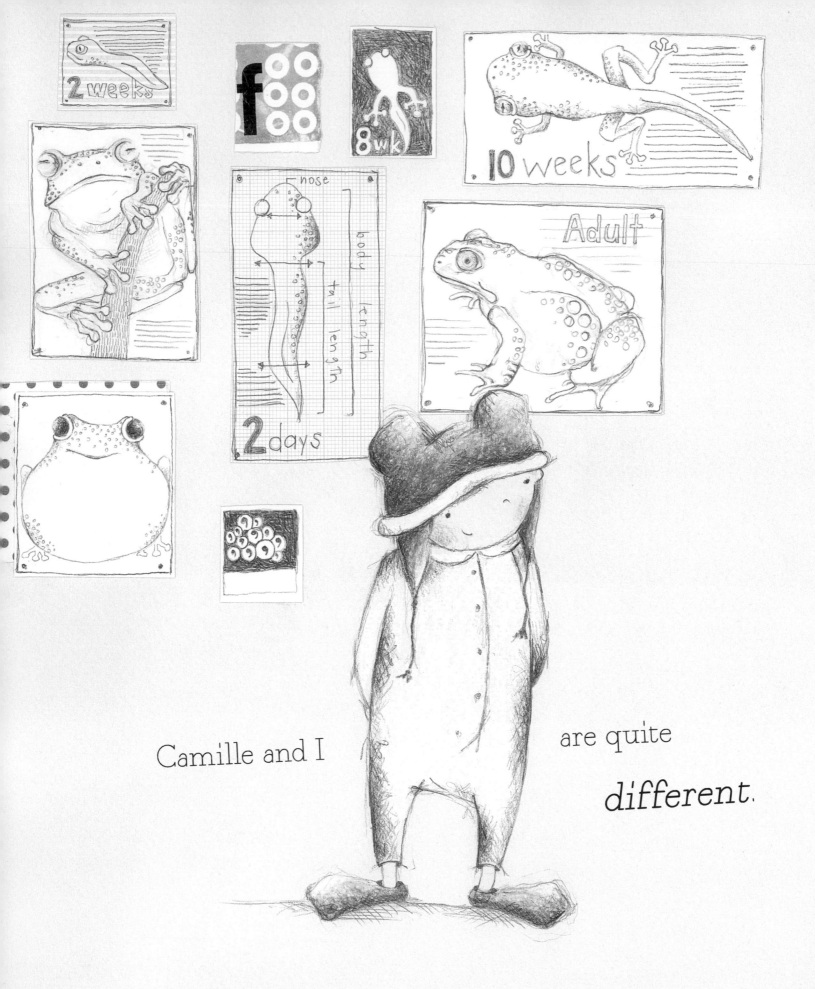

Camille and I are quite **different**.

Maybe that's why
I like her so much.

Camille loves math so much that some days

she only talks in **numbers**.

So far I've worked out

that **23** is *yes*

and **17** is **no**.

And when she starts singing

her **six** times tables,

I know it's time for a *snack*.

When I first met Camille

I was dressed as a cat.

Dodie would **bark** at me

the *whole way* to school

and the *whole way*

back home again.

It was more attention than I wanted.

After watching Dodie chase me

day *in* and day **out**

for **exactly 11** days,

Camille called me over

and *whispered* in my ear.

She suggested I

try another

animal.

Finding the **right** animal for me

wasn't easy.

 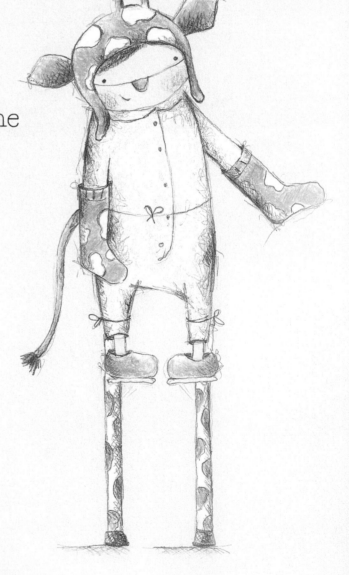

It was Camille who *finally* gave me the idea of...

a frog.

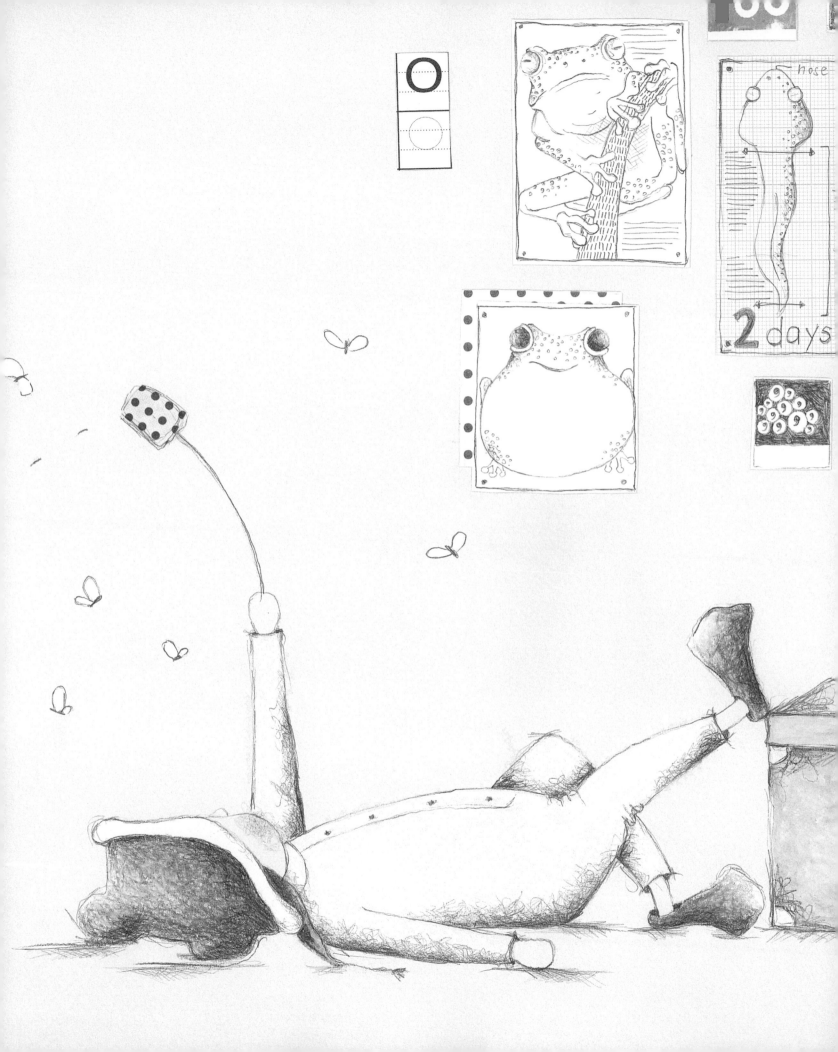

10 weeks

nose

body length

tail length

Adult

2 days

Frogs are not

solitary creatures.

I decided I needed

a *friend*.

Camille agreed to help.

At first we worked together well.

Camille did the measuring and I did the sewing.

But putting together her costume was taking

a little *longer* than expected.

Camille started singing

her **six** times tables . . .

I was getting confused
with the
measurements.
Camille just
wouldn't stand still.

She sang her **six** times tables

louder and **louder**.

Suddenly,

and without thinking,

I shouted . . .

Camille picked up her bag

and her stopwatch

and went *home*.

Without Camille

8

I felt *alone*.

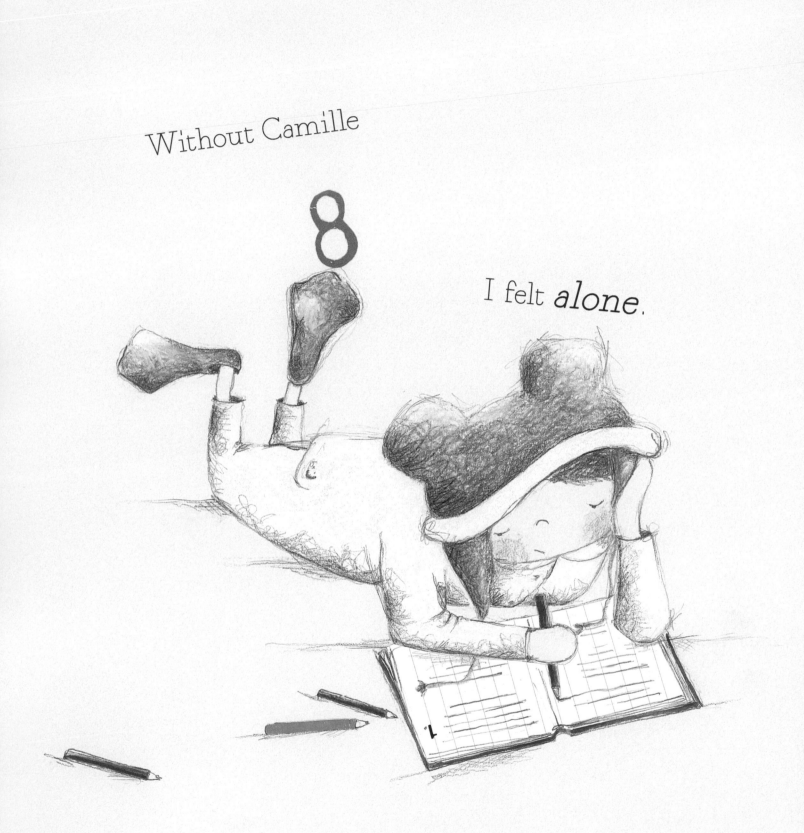

I decided to write a list:

The Pros and Cons of Being a Frog

Pros
1. My friend Camille gave me the idea

2. I'm less likely to be chased by a dog

3. Being in a frog costume makes me feel brave

Cons
1. Not everyone loves wearing a frog costume as much as I do

2. If you start getting **bossy** about your frog costume then your friend will get up and leave

3. A frog is **not** a solitary creature, so it's no fun for a frog if his friend gets up and leaves

I went to

find Camille

to say *sorry*.

Everywhere I looked,

all I could see were numbers—

but no Camille.

Just as I was about to *give up*

I heard a **sound** coming

toward me . . .

flip flap

flip flap

flip flap . . .

"I'm sorry," I said.

Camille and I are quite *different*.

That's **why** I like her so much.